For Ollie, Alice, Lexie and Jack – S.P-H.

For Theodore, my little digger expert! E.E.

READY, STEADY, DIG!

HODDER CHILDREN'S BOOKS

First published in Great Britain in 2015 by Hodder and Stoughton
This paperback edition published in 2016

3 5 7 9 10 8 6 4

A CIP catalogue record for this book is available from the British Libra

ISBN: 978 1 444 92358 2

Printed in China

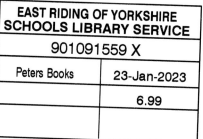

Hodder Children's Books
An imprint of Hachette Children's Group
Part of Hodder and Stoughton
Carmelite House
50 Victoria Embankment
London EC4Y 0DZ

An Hachette UK Company
www.hachette.co.uk

www.hachettechildrens.co.uk

Hodder
Children's
Books

Ready, Steady, DIG!

Smriti Prasadam-Halls   Ed Eaves

Let's go to work, Construction Crew!
Time to see what you can do.
Put your toughness to the test,
Build, build, build your very best.

Motors starting, BRMM **BRMM BRMM!**
Engines revving, **VRMM VRMM VRMM!**

Get in gear, don't be slow!
Ready, steady... **OFF WE GO!**

CONNOR CRANE is at the ready,
With his steel chain holding steady.

High up hanging,
CLINGING, CLANGING.

His wrecking ball goes BASH, BASH, BASH!
Ready, steady...
SMASH, SMASH, CRASH!

DUMPER DAVE is big and tough,
For any job, he's strong enough.
CREEPING, CRAWLING,
HEAVING,
HAULING.

Rubble in his sturdy skip. Now, ready, steady...

TIP, TIP, TIP!

MIXER MILLIE spins and hums,
Cement is churning in her drum.

BARREL WHIRLING,
CONCRETE SWIRLING.

RAVI ROLLER takes his spot,
Squashing tarmac, wet and hot.

SQUELCHING,

SPLATTERING,

SQUEEZING,

FLATTENING.

Press it smooth, no bumps or holes,
Ready, steady...

ROLL,
ROLL, ROLL!

DOUG THE DIGGER

loves to dig,
Gobbling earth,
however big.

MUNCHING, CRUNCHING,
SCRAPING, SCRUNCHING.

...OOPS!

Oh dear, oh dear, what bad luck,
Doug the Digger's

STUCK, STUCK,

STUCK!

He gives a **YELL,**
he gives a **SHOUT,**
Can anybody get him out?

ALL his friends roar into action,
Wheels a-turning, gaining traction.

WELL DONE, TEAM! All safely back!
Now let's keep going, stay on track.
Complete the project, brick by brick,
And get the job done,

DOUBLE QUICK.

Shunting, shifting,
loading, lifting,

Using all your strength and skill.
READY, STEADY...

BUILD,

BUILD,

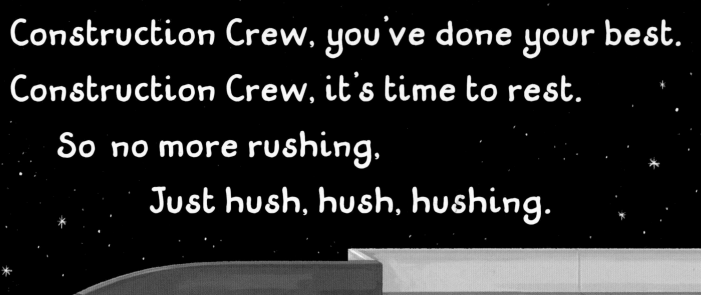

Construction Crew, you've done your best.
Construction Crew, it's time to rest.
So no more rushing,
Just hush, hush, hushing.

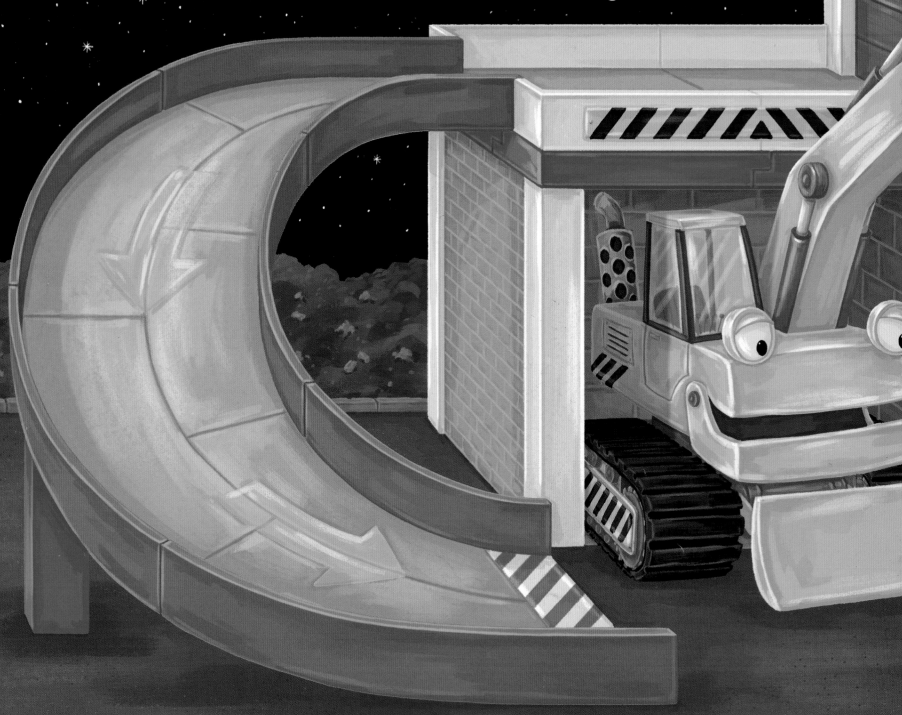

Not another HONK or BEEP...

READY, STEADY...
time to SLEEP! s s s s

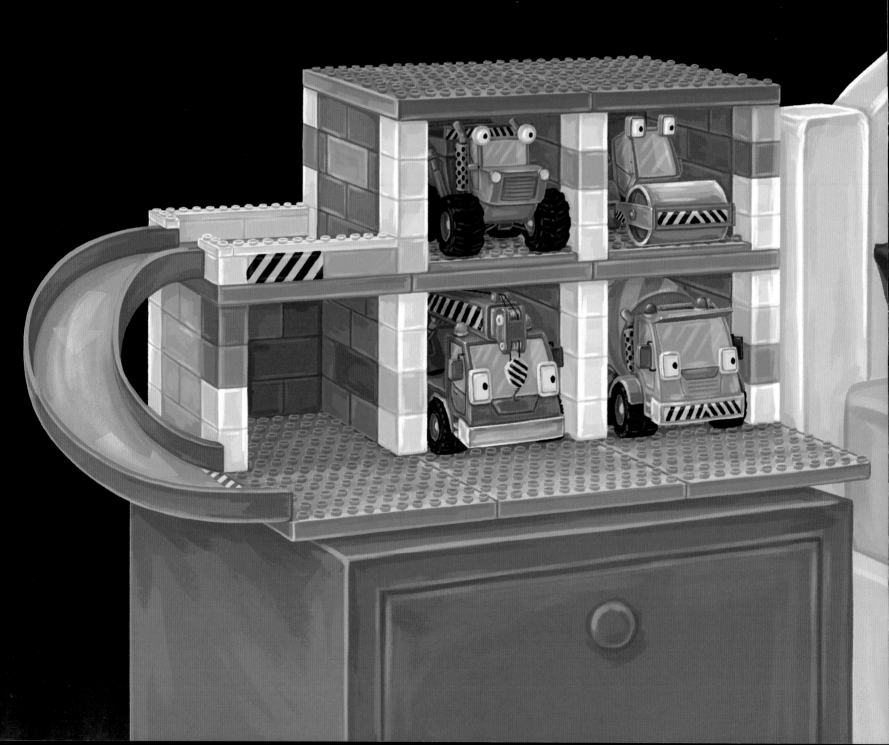

h h h h h h h h h h h h h h h h
h

Also by
Smriti Prasadam-Halls
and Ed Eaves: